freedom

summer

freedom

written by Deborah Wiles

summer

illustrated by Jerome Lagarrigue

An Anne Schwartz Book
ATHENEUM BOOKS FOR YOUNG READERS
New York   London   Toronto   Sydney   Singapore

For the children of the Movement and for Butch, who believed
—D. W.

Atheneum Books for Young Readers
An imprint of Simon & Schuster Children's Publishing Division
1230 Avenue of the Americas
New York, New York 10020

Book design by Ann Bobco

The text of this book is set in Centaur MT.

Printed in Hong Kong

10 9 8 7 6 5 4 3 2

Library of Congress Cataloging-in-Publication Data
Wiles, Deborah.
Freedom summer / by Deborah Wiles; illustrated by Jerome Lagarrigue.
p. cm.
Summary: In 1964, Joe is pleased that a new law will allow his best friend John Henry, who is colored, to share the town pool
and other public places with him, but he is dismayed to find that prejudice still exists.
ISBN 0-689-83016-5
1. Afro-Americans—Juvenile fiction. [1. Afro-Americans—Fiction. 2. Race relations—Fiction. 3. Friendship—Fiction.]
I. Lagarrigue, Jerome, ill. II. Title.
PZ7.W6474Fr   2001   [Fic]—dc21   98-52805

Acknowledgements:

I'm grateful for Anne Schwartz's sensibilities and Caitlin Van Dusen's assistance; for Deborah Hopkinson's question, "What
story do you really want to tell?"; for the support of my family, my fellow writers and the Minis; and for the talents of
Jerome Lagarrigue, the enthusiasm of my librarian friends at the C. Burr Artz library in Frederick, Maryland, and the special
contributions of James Walker, Chrystal Jeter, and Fredrick and Patricia McKissack.   —D. W.

A NOTE ABOUT THE TEXT

In the early 1960s the American South had long been a place where black Americans could not drink from the same drinking fountains as whites, attend the same schools, or enjoy the same public areas. Then the Civil Rights Act of 1964 became law and stated that "All persons shall be entitled to the full and equal enjoyment" of any public place, regardless of ". . . race, color, religion, or national origin."

I was born a white child in Mobile, Alabama, and spent summers visiting my beloved Mississippi relatives. When the Civil Rights Act was passed, the town pool closed. So did the roller rink and the ice-cream parlor. Rather than lawfully giving blacks the same rights and freedoms as whites, many southern businesses chose to shut their doors in protest. Some of them closed forever.

Also in the summer of 1964, civil rights workers in Mississippi organized "Freedom Summer," a movement to register black Americans to vote. It was a time of great racial violence and change. That was the summer I began to pay attention: I noticed that black Americans used back doors, were waited on only after every white had been helped, and were treated poorly, all because of the color of their skin . . . and no matter what any law said. I realized that a white person openly having a black friend, and vice versa, could be a dangerous thing. I couldn't get these thoughts and images out of my mind, and I wondered what it must be like to be a black child my age. I dreamed about changing things, and yet I wondered what any child—black or white—could do.

This story grew out of my feelings surrounding that time. It is fiction, but based on real events.

John Henry Waddell is my best friend.

His mama works for my mama.

Her name is Annie Mae.

Every morning at eight o'clock Annie Mae

steps off the county bus

and walks up the long hill to my house.

If it's summer, John Henry is step-step-stepping-it

right beside her.

We like to help Annie Mae.

We shell butter beans. We sweep the front porch.

We let the cats in, then chase the cats out of the house

until Annie Mae says,

"Shoo! Enough of you two! Go play!"

We shoot marbles in the dirt

until we're too hot to be alive.

Then we yell, "Last one in is a rotten egg!"

and run straight for Fiddler's Creek.

John Henry swims better than anybody I know.

He crawls like a catfish, blows bubbles like a swamp monster,

but he doesn't swim in the town pool with me.

He's not allowed.

So we dam the creek with rocks and sticks

to make a swimming spot,

then holler and jump in, wearing only our skin.

John Henry's skin is the color of
browned butter.
He smells like pine needles after a
good rain.
My skin is the color of the pale
moths that dance around the porch
light at night.
John Henry says I smell like a
just-washed sock.
"This means war!" I shout.
We churn that water into a
white hurricane and laugh until
our sides hurt.
Then we float on our backs and
spout like whales.
"I'm gonna be a fireman
when I grow up," I say.
"Me, too," says John Henry.

I have two nickels for ice pops,

so we put on our clothes and walk to town.

John Henry doesn't come with me through the front door

of Mr. Mason's General Store.

He's not allowed.

"How you doin', Young Joe?" asks Mr. Mason. He winks and says,

"You gonna eat these all by yourself?"

My heart does a quick-beat.

"I got one for a friend," I say, and scoot out the door.

"Yessir, it's mighty hot out there!" Mr. Mason calls after me.

"I love ice pops," says John Henry.

"Me, too," I say.

Annie Mae makes dinner for my family every night.

She creams the corn and rolls the biscuits.

Daddy stirs his iced tea and says, "The town pool opens tomorrow

to everybody under the sun, no matter what color."

"That's the new law," Mama tells me.

She helps my plate with peas and says, "It's the way it's going to be now—

Everybody Together—

lunch counters, rest rooms, drinking fountains, too."

I wiggle in my chair like a doodlebug.

"I got to be excused!" I shout, and I run into the kitchen

to tell John Henry.

"I'm gonna swim in the town pool!" he hollers. "Is it deep?"

"REAL deep," I tell him. "And the water's so clear,
 you can jump to the bottom and open your eyes and still see."

"Let's be the first ones there," says John Henry.

"I'll bring my good-luck nickel, and we can dive for it."

Next morning, as soon as the sun peeks into the sky,

here comes my best friend, John Henry Waddell,

run-run-running to meet me.

"Let's go!" he yells, "I got my nickel,"

and I run right with him,

all the way to the town swimming pool.

We race each other over the last hill and . . .

we stop.

County dump trucks are here.

They grind and back up to the empty pool.

Workers rake steaming asphalt into the hole where

sparkling clean water used to be.

One of them is John Henry's big brother, Will Rogers.

We start to call to him, "What happened?"

but he sees us first and points back on down the road—

it means "Git on home!"

But our feet feel stuck, we can't budge.

So we hunker in the tall weeds and watch all morning

until the pool is filled with hot, spongy tar.

Ssssss! Smoky steam rises in the air.

Workers tie planks to their shoes and stomp on the blacktop

to make it smooth.

Will Rogers heaves his shovel into the back of an empty truck

and climbs up with the other workers.

His face is like a storm cloud, and

I know this job has made him angry.

"Let's go!" a boss man shouts, and

the trucks rumble-slam down the road.

It's so quiet now, we can hear the breeze
whisper through the grass.
We sit on the diving board
and stare at the tops of the silver ladders
sticking up from the tar.
My heart beats hard in my chest.
John Henry's voice shakes.
"White folks don't want colored folks
in their pool."
"You're wrong, John Henry," I say,
but I know he's right.
"Let's go back to Fiddler's Creek," I say.
"I didn't want to swim in this old pool
anyway."

John Henry's eyes fill up with angry tears.

"I did," he says. "I wanted to swim in this pool.

I want to do everything you can do."

I don't know what to say,

but as we walk back to town,

my head starts to pop with new ideas.

I want to go to the Dairy Dip with John Henry,

sit down and share root beer floats.

I want us to go to the picture show, buy popcorn,

and watch the movie together.

I want to see this town with John Henry's eyes.

We stop in front of Mr. Mason's store.

I jam my hands into my pockets

while my mind searches for words to put with my new ideas.

My fingers close around two nickels.

"Want to get an ice pop?"

John Henry wipes his eyes and takes a breath.

"I want to pick it out myself."

I swallow hard and my heart says yes.

"Let's do that," I say.

I give John Henry one of my nickels.

He shakes his head. "I got my own."

We look at each other.

Then we walk through the front door together.